Only at Night

For Dolores García Albarracin
Directora del Colegio Vera Cruz, Vitoria, hasta 2010.

Only at Night

Keva Connolly   Javi Kintana

I'm afraid of rats and bats,
tigers, and loud noises, I don't like wolves,
owls or snakes that are poisonous.

I'm afraid it might rain and I'll sink in a puddle,
my head starts to wander and I'm left in a muddle.

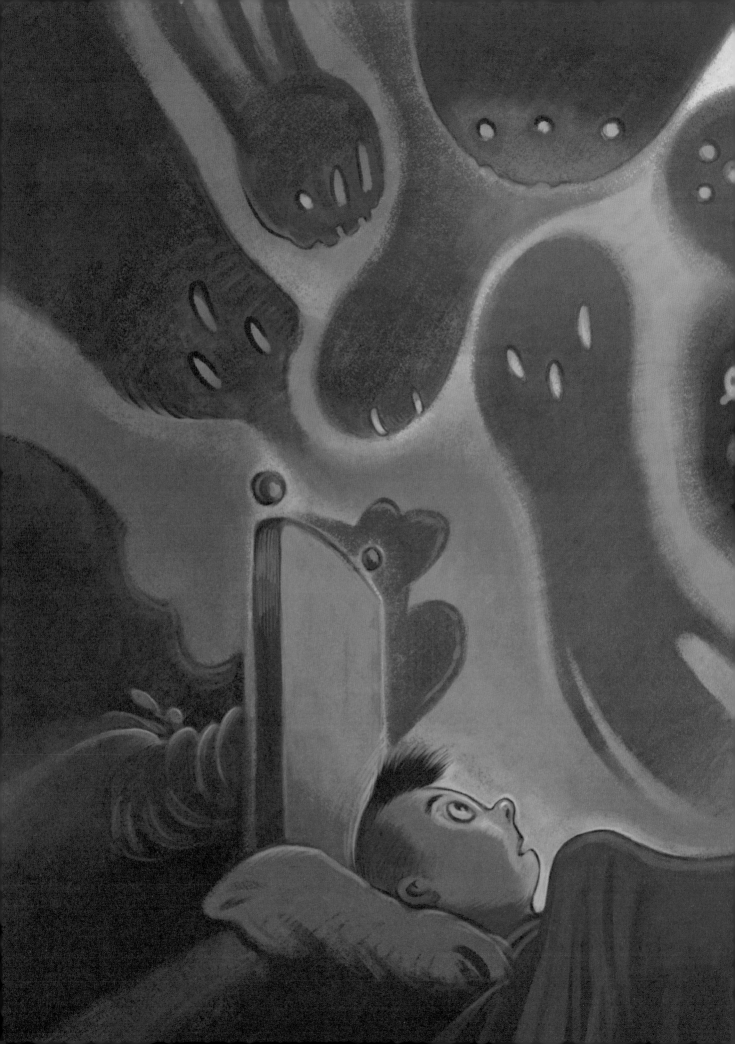

My bedroom is dark and
I can't see the wall, that could
be a monster or a ghost,
pale and tall.

Could be a clown in a hat, his face frowning, an orphaned cat with fleas, hunched over and growling.

Huge horns on a goat
or a horse with no head,
I pull up the covers and
sink down in the bed.

Storms rage, lightning flashes,
I count the seconds between bangs
and crashes.
They say if you count them you can tell
if it´s moving, I prick up my ear, the distance
is soothing.
The storm will move on, the calm will
take over, I lower the blanket from
my ear to my shoulder.

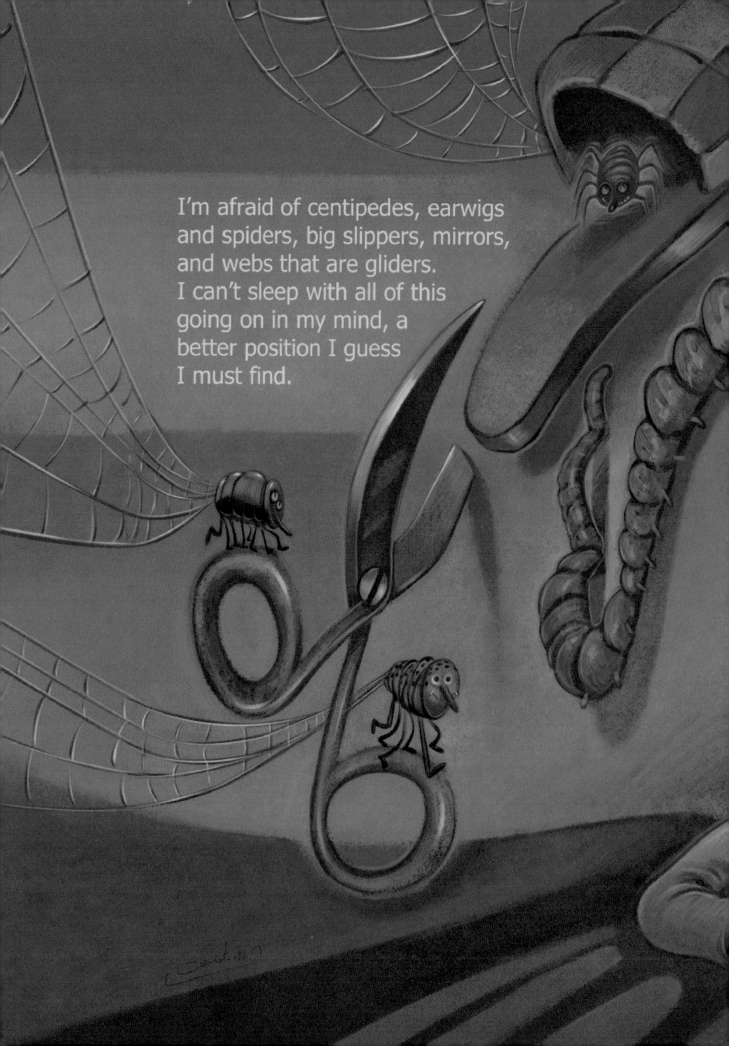

I'm afraid of centipedes, earwigs and spiders, big slippers, mirrors, and webs that are gliders. I can't sleep with all of this going on in my mind, a better position I guess I must find.

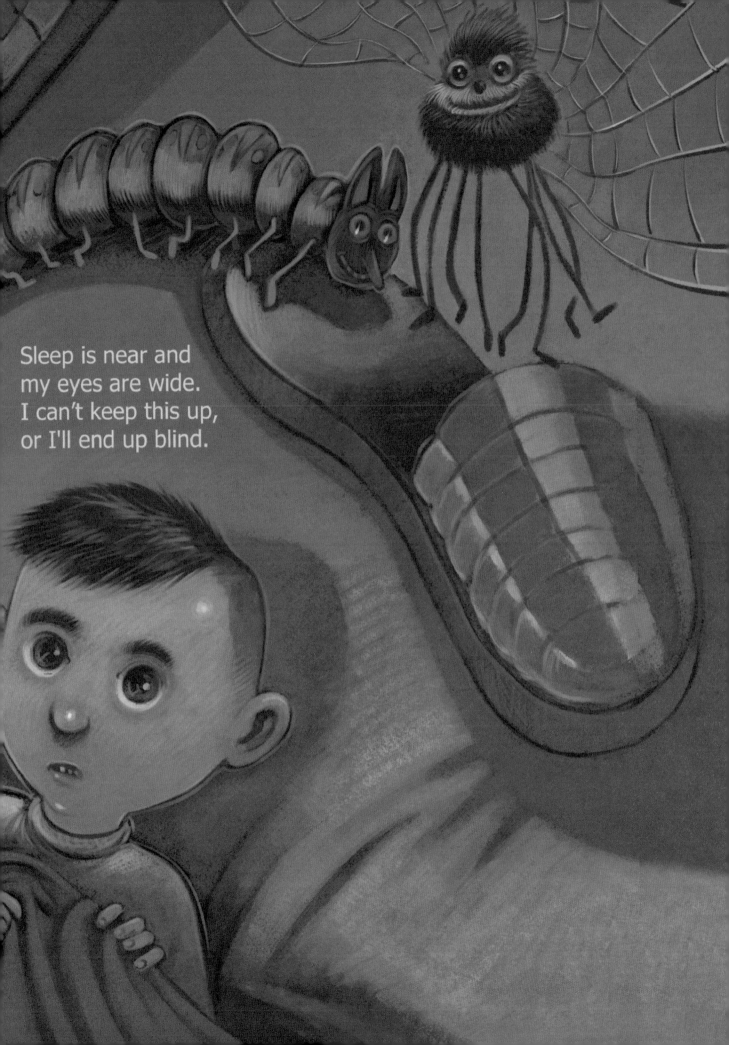

Sleep is near and
my eyes are wide.
I can't keep this up,
or I'll end up blind.

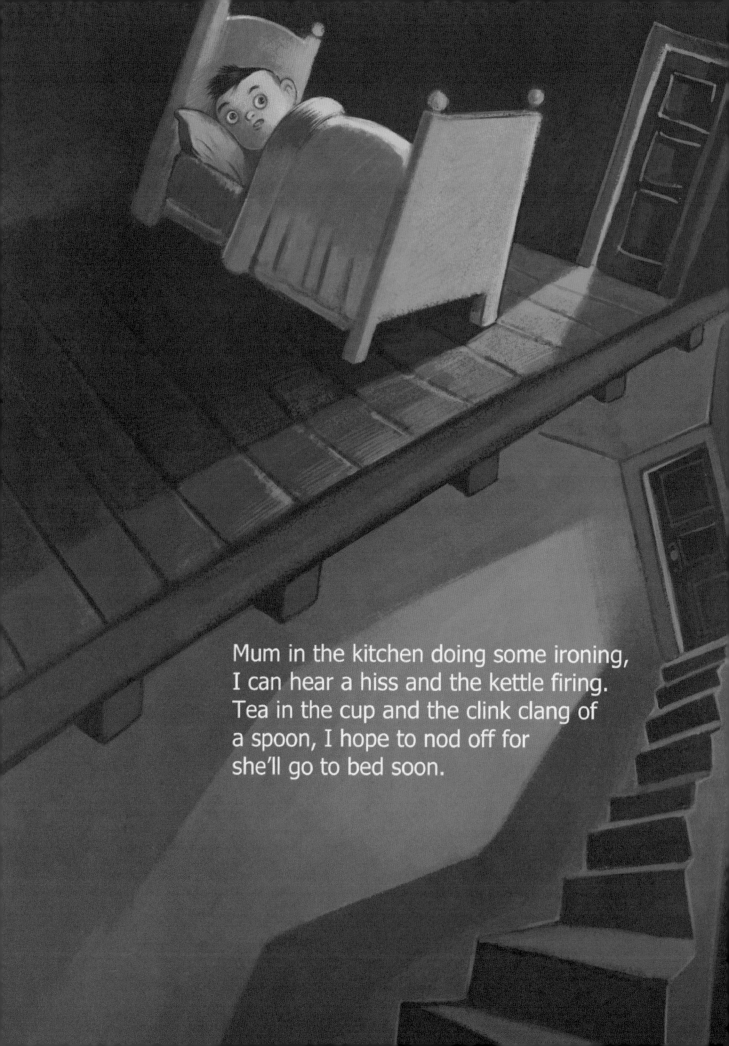

Mum in the kitchen doing some ironing,
I can hear a hiss and the kettle firing.
Tea in the cup and the clink clang of
a spoon, I hope to nod off for
she'll go to bed soon.

I'm nearly eight and I should be braver,
but even so, these fears will not waver.
I'll stay here till morning, not move or twitch,
I can only hope Dad leaves on a light switch.

As always I awake, my room I search,
not a thing has been moved from a shelf
or a perch.
I remember the fear from the images I make,
but only at night they keep me awake.
By day these things don't bother me I find,
only at night they prey on my mind.

Maybe I'll start back to counting sheep,
it helps me get quickly off to sleep.
So tonight when I go, I'll think of Bo-Peep,
not the wolf, not the fox, but of soft white fleece.

What scares you at night?

Printed in Great Britain
by Amazon

83478706R00016